Badger at Sandy Ridge Road

I dedicate this book to my dear friend, Rev. Philip W. Brady, M.S. Ed., with love and fond memories of the old days in Greenwich—K.D.

To S^2 with love forever—K^2

Published by Soundprints Division of Trudy Corporation, Norwalk, Connecticut.

Book design: Shields & Partners, Westport, CT
Book layout: Marcin D. Pilchowski
Editor: Laura Gates Galvin

First Edition 2005
10 9 8 7 6 5 4 3 2 1
Printed in Singapore

Acknowledgements:
    Our very special thanks to Dr. Don E. Wilson of the Department of Systematic Biology at the Smithsonian Institution's National Museum of Natural History for his curatorial review.
    Soundprints would also like to thank Ellen Nanney and Katie Mann at the Smithsonian Institution's Office of Product Development and Licensing for their help in the creation of this book.

Library of Congress Cataloging-in-Publication Data is on file with the publisher and the Library of Congress.

Badger at Sandy Ridge Road

by Katacha Díaz

Illustrated by Kristin Kest

Late on a warm spring afternoon, swallows fly across the sky behind the old adobe house on Sandy Ridge Road. Hummingbirds dart from one prickly pear blossom to another for a sip of sweet nectar before they settle in for the long night.

Soon the sun sets and the desert's nighttime dwellers begin their activities. A badger stirs from a safe sleep in her underground burrow.

5

Badger wriggles out of her sleeping nest. She crawls through the pitch-black tunnel, making her way up to the entrance hole. Then she pops her furry head out and sniffs the cool nighttime air. This is Badger's favorite time!

As the silvery moon rises, Badger spots a
wood rat carrying a piece of cactus in its mouth.
Badger twitches her nose. She sniffs the
air, looks around, and listens. And, in the
distance, she hears the howls of
hungry coyote pups.

Keeping a sharp watch, Badger looks around to make sure there are no predators lurking about in the yard. Slowly, she lifts herself out of the hole and plops her fat, furry tummy down to rest on the soft, sandy soil.

Badger waddles across the desert toward the moonlit courtyard, but stops when she spots a jackrabbit. Badger stands very still. The jackrabbit senses that danger is near. He jumps and runs very fast into the nighttime desert. The jackrabbit would make a tasty meal for Badger, but not tonight!

Most nights, Badger digs a new, shallow burrow for sleeping, hunting, and storing food, leaving behind a trail of freshly dug burrows near the backyard. But tonight is different. Badger is searching for that special place to dig her nesting chamber. She is going to have pups soon and she needs a bigger place with extra rooms to raise her babies comfortably.

A Gila monster moves slowly and makes its way to the rocks by the old wagon wheel. Since the Gila monster's bite is deadly, Badger stands very still. She watches as the large, poisonous lizard chews on the rattlesnake eggs it found under the rocks. The rattlesnake eggs would make a good snack for Badger, but not tonight!

Badger waddles across the path to the stream behind the house. She turns and looks in all directions and listens for any sounds of danger.

Badger sees several holes. She sniffs the scent of ground squirrels. This is the perfect spot for her nesting chamber! She lowers her head and, with her long, thick front claws, she begins to dig a hole.

Suddenly, Badger hears rustling sounds coming from behind the bushes. She stops digging and listens, her small ears turning in all directions. Then she notices the leaves of the bush move. Badger knows there is something hiding there, but will she be fast enough to catch whatever it is?

In the dark, Badger sees a pair of eyes peeking from behind the bush. Then an owl hoots and gets her attention. As Badger waddles over to the bush, the owl flies off into the moonlit sky and the mouse that was hiding in the bushes scurries away.

Owls and mice make good snacks for Badger, but not tonight!

23

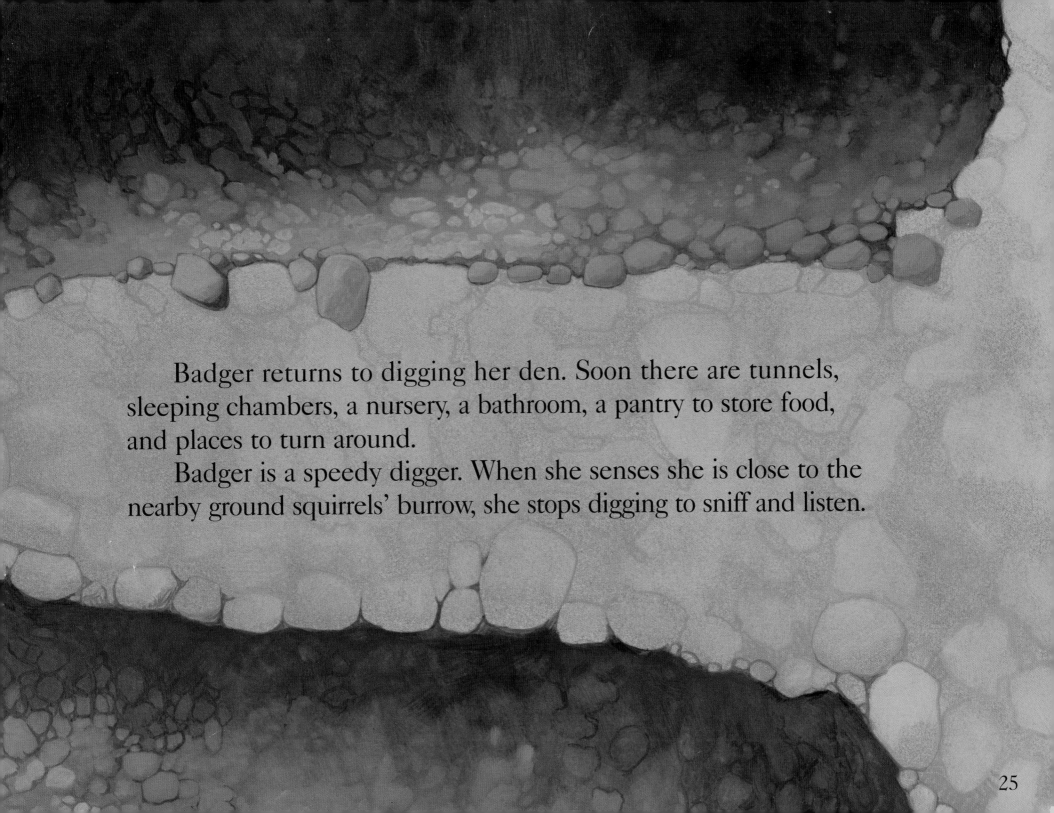

Badger returns to digging her den. Soon there are tunnels, sleeping chambers, a nursery, a bathroom, a pantry to store food, and places to turn around.

Badger is a speedy digger. When she senses she is close to the nearby ground squirrels' burrow, she stops digging to sniff and listen.

Using her long, thick front claws, Badger quickly digs a connecting tunnel to the burrow where the ground squirrels are fast asleep. Just as Badger reaches over to grab a ground squirrel, it leaps away and runs up another tunnel to the entrance hole, escaping into the desert.

Ground squirrels are one of Badger's favorite foods. They would make a tasty meal for Badger, but not tonight!

Badger works hard throughout the night to prepare for the arrival of her pups. Now she needs to look for something soft to line her pups' nest.

Across the backyard, near the clothesline, Badger spots a new crop of grasses. They are soft and the perfect material to line her nest. When her pups are born, they will have a soft, snug and safe place to sleep.

In the predawn hours of the morning, Badger gives birth to four tiny pups. The babies are born with their eyes shut and no teeth. Their tiny bodies are covered with a soft, fuzzy fur.

Since the pups are born helpless, Badger will spend most of her time underground in her den feeding them milk, grooming them and keeping them warm.

For the next six weeks, Badger will guard her pups and keep them safe in their nest deep underground behind the old adobe house on Sandy Ridge Road.

About the North American Badger

The North American badger lives in farmlands, mountains, deserts, and grasslands from southern Canada to southern Mexico. Badgers spend a good part of their time digging in and crawling out of their burrows.

Although badgers have short legs, they are speedy diggers and in a matter of minutes can dig down six feet or more. Badgers use their short, powerful front legs and their strong claws like a shovel to break ground and dig. They use their flat body and back legs to move loose dirt out of the way.

The badger is a nocturnal animal. It stays underground in its burrow during the daylight hours and goes out at night when it's safe to dig a new burrow and find food.

Adult badgers live alone, except at mating time in late summer. One to five pups are born in March or April. The adult female stays in one burrow until the pups are old enough to venture out with her to look for a place to dig a new burrow. When the pups are four months old, they leave their mother and live on their own.

Glossary

adobe: Sun-dried mud and straw bricks.

burrow: An underground hole dug by an animal, used for sleeping, giving birth, hunting, and storing food.

jackrabbit: A large North American hare, similar to a rabbit, but with very long ears and long hindlegs.

nesting chamber: A grass-lined room at the end of the burrow used by the female badger to give birth and care for her pups.

predators: Animals that hunt and eat other animals.

wood rat: A rodent, similar to a mouse, that scurries about the Southwestern desert at night looking for objects to add to its nest.

Points of Interest in This Book

pp. 04-05: black-chinned hummingbirds
pp. 06-07: shining leaf chafer beetle
pp. 08-09: desert kangaroo rat
pp. 12-13: blacktail jackrabbit
pp. 16-17: Gila monster
pp. 22-23: northern pygmy owl
pp. 26-27: thirteen-lined ground squirrel
pp. 30-31: badger pups